This Little Story
belongs to

A catalogue record for this book is available
from the British Library

Published by Ladybird Books Ltd
A subsidiary of the Penguin Group
A Pearson Company
© LADYBIRD BOOKS LTD MCMXCV, MCMXCVII

LADYBIRD and the device of a Ladybird are trademarks of
Ladybird Books Ltd Loughborough Leicestershire UK

Little Red Car

by Nicola Baxter
illustrated by Colin Reeder
and David Melling

"Happy beep, beepity, BEEP! Happy beep, beepity, BEEP!" sang the Little Red Car one sunny morning. "Now why do I keep beeping that song? Is it a special sort of day today?"

Just then Mike-the-Mechanic's pick-up truck went clanking past. "Hurry up, Little Red Car!" called Mike-the-Mechanic. "Gary-at-the-Garage is expecting you *any minute now*!"

"Well wiggle my wipers!" thought the Little Red Car. "I can't be late for my service! I *knew* something important was happening today."

She didn't waste one more minute. With a beep, beepity, BEEP! she whizzed off down the road.

Brrrm vrrrm! The Little Red Car raced round the corner. "I'll be there in no time," she thought.

But suddenly…

What was that ahead in the lane? A tall truck full of blown-up balloons was chugging slowly along.

"Beep, beepity, BEEP! Excuse me!" cried the Little Red Car. "I'm late for a Very Important Appointment. Can't you go any faster?"

But the truck was going as fast as it could. It just chugged steadily on.

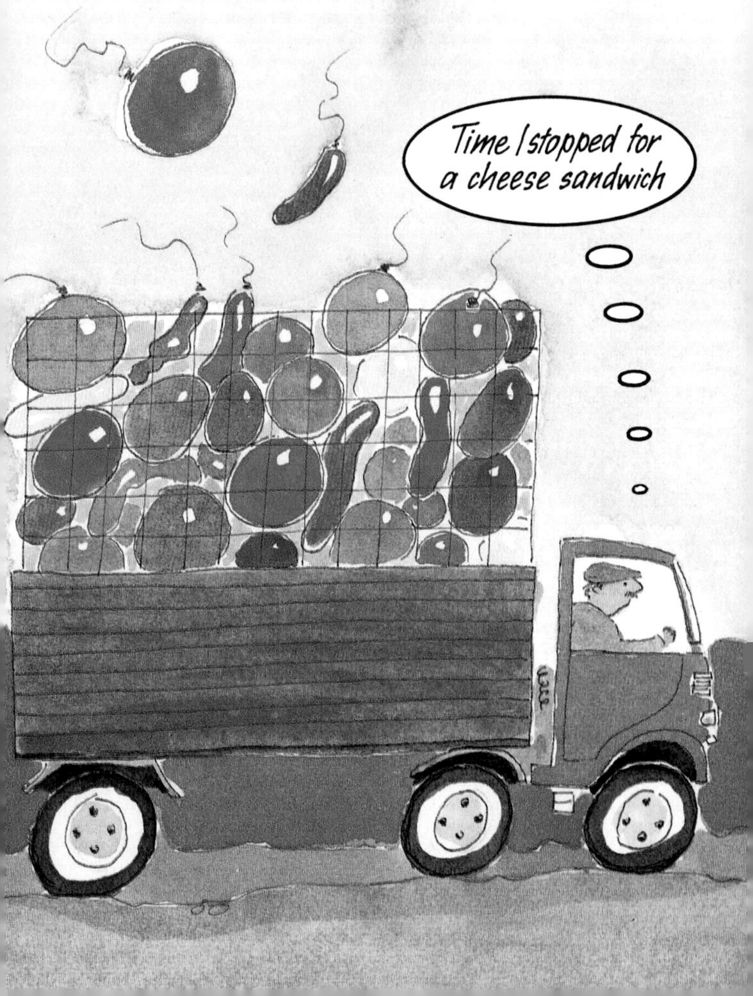
Time I stopped for
a cheese sandwich

The Little Red Car brrrmed and beeped behind the truck until... *at last*... it pulled into a lay-by. "*Brrrm vrrrm!* Watch my wheels whizz now!" said the Little Red Car.

But suddenly...

What was that on the road ahead? A baker's van was crawling carefully along.

"Beep, beepity, BEEP! Hurry up!" called the Little Red Car. "Is that as fast as you can go? I've got a Most Important Meeting!"

But the van came to a bumpety bump bit of road and went *even* slower.

The Little Red Car brrrmed and beeped behind the van until… *at last*… the road widened and she could pass. "*Brrrm vrrrm!* You won't see me for dust!" said the Little Red Car.

But suddenly…

What was that ahead? A blue truck loaded *full* of tooters and hooters and bangers and clangers was trundling along.

"Beep, beepity, BEEP! Get a move on!" cried the Little Red Car. "A snail could go faster than this!"

But the blue truck, with its heavy load, was going as fast as it could. It just kept trundling along.

The Little Red Car brrrmed and beeped behind the blue truck until… *at last*… it pulled into a gateway and she could zoom past. *"Brrrm vrrrm!* Full steam ahead!" said the Little Red Car.

But suddenly…

What was that right across the road? An Extra Wide Load was moving slowly along.

"Beep, beepity, BEEP! Speed it up!" yelled the Little Red Car. "You lumbering great lorry, can't you wait until *I'm* not on the road?"

But a policeman on a motorbike was travelling with the lorry. Ooops! The Little Red Car went rather quiet.

The Little Red Car followed the Extra Wide Load until… *at last*… the policeman stopped the traffic and waved her past. *"Brrrm vrrrm!* I'm the fastest thing on four wheels!" said the Little Red Car.

But suddenly…

What was that blocking the road? A battered old bus full of children was rumbling along.

"Beep, beepity, BEEP! I don't believe it!" groaned the Little Red Car.

But the battered old bus just kept rumbling along.

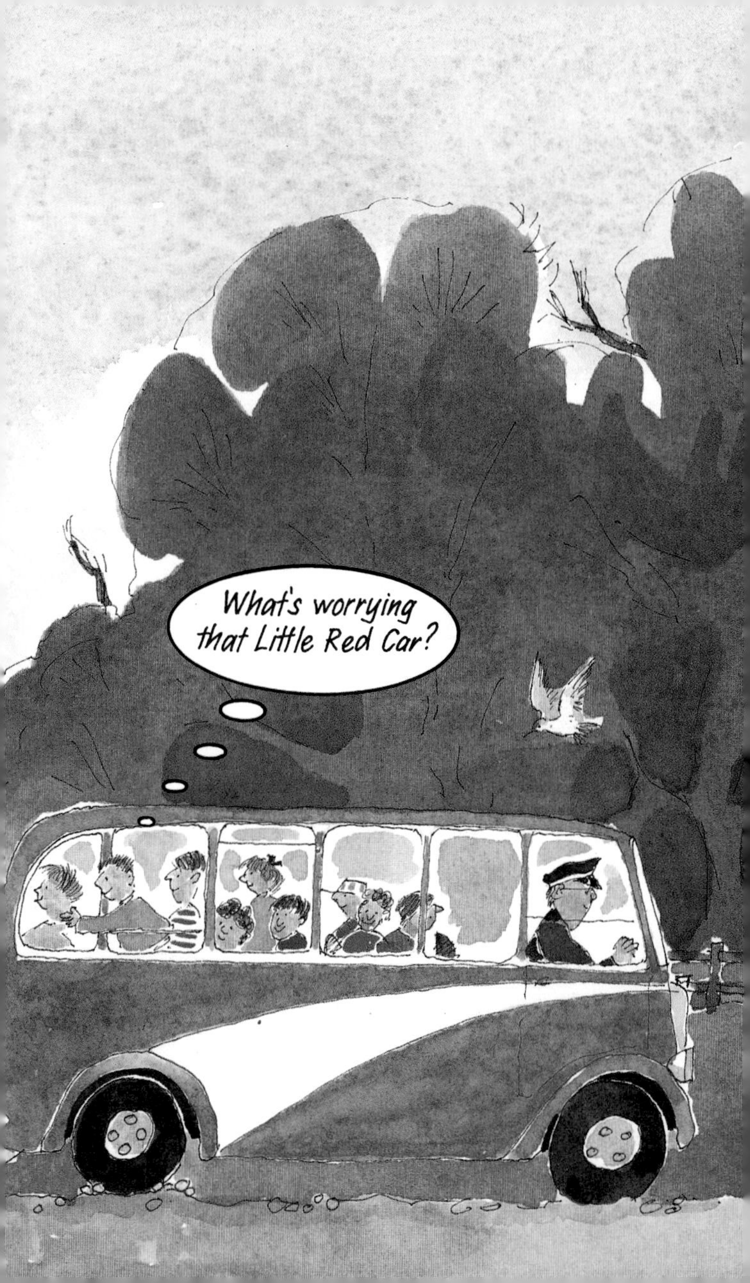
What's worrying that Little Red Car?

The Little Red Car brrrmed and beeped behind the battered old bus until… *at last*… it stopped outside a café and she could dash past. "*Brrrm vrrrm*! What a relief! I'm nearly there!" said the Little Red Car.

But suddenly…

Who was this in the middle of the road? A clown on one wheel was wobbling along.

"Beep, beepity, BEEP! Keep to the side!" shouted the Little Red Car. "I'm meeting a friend just round the next bend!"

Ooo… er… The clown on one wheel wobbled and wiggled and sat down with a BUMP in a bush.

At last! The Little Red Car brrrmed and beeped her way past the clown. "*Brrrm vrrrm!* Nothing can stop me now!" she said.

But suddenly…

What was happening to the Little Red Car? With a *futt*, *futt*, *putt-putt-putt*, she came to a silent…

standing…

stop.

"Beep, beepity, BEEP! I've run out of petrol! I *thought* I had a funny feeling in my fuel tank," said the Little Red Car wearily.

The Little Red Car sat miserably by the side of the road. She didn't brrrm or vrrrm or beep.

But suddenly…

Dring, DRING! The clown wobbled past on his one wheel.

Barp, BARP! The battered old bus rumbled past and all the children smiled and waved.

Toot, TOOT! The Extra Wide Load *and* the policeman moved slowly past.

Honk, HONK! The blue truck loaded full of tooters and hooters and bangers and clangers trundled past.

Peep, PEEP! The baker's van crawled carefully past.

Boop, BOOP! Last of all the tall truck full of blown-up balloons chugged slowly past.

Slow as a snail? Huh!

"I've been very silly," thought the Little Red Car. "With all my beeping and brrrming and vrrrming, I'm not surprised nobody wants to help me."

But suddenly…

Who was this wobbling on one wheel down the road? The clown was bringing a can of petrol and he was smiling all over his face.

"Come on, Little Red Car," he said. "Gary-at-the-Garage says we can't start without *you*!"

In no time at all the Little Red Car was filled up with petrol and…*at last*… she was on her way again.

And suddenly...

There was the truck and the baker's van and the blue truck and the Extra Wide Load and the battered old bus. And there were balloons and a birthday cake and a band and a bouncy castle *and* the policeman and the children and Gary-at-the-Garage with a great big smile on his face!

"Happy birthday, Little Red Car!" he grinned. "We couldn't start your party without *you*!" And everybody sang…

"Happy dring, barpety toot!
Happy honk, peepity boop!
Happy beep, beepity birthday,
Happy birthday to you!"